THE SCRUFFS

SHOWTIME!

HANNAH SHAW

KT-157-057

Scholastic Children's Books
An imprint of Scholastic Ltd
Euston House, 24 Eversholt Street, London, NW1 1DB, UK
Registered office: Westfield Road, Southam, Warwickshire, CV47 0RA
SCHOLASTIC and associated logos are trademarks and/or
registered trademarks of Scholastic Inc.

First published in the UK by Scholastic Ltd, 2017

Text and illustration copyright © Hannah Shaw, 2017

The right of Hannah Shaw to be identified as the author
and illustrator of this work has been asserted by her.

ISBN 978 1407 16442 7

A CIP catalogue record for this book
is available from the British Library.

Printed by CPI Group (UK) Ltd, Croydon, CR0 4YY

Papers used by Scholastic Children's Books are made
from wood grown in sustainable forests.

1 3 5 7 9 10 8 6 4 2

www.scholastic.co.uk

THE SCRUFFS

SHOWTIME!

Chapter One
LATE AT THE FETE

It was a glorious day for the Much Muddling town fete. The sun was shining, a brass band was playing *Oom-pah-pah-pah!* and the playing field was teeming. There were people sipping tea in their best summer clothes, throwing balls at coconuts, tripping over guy ropes, and gambling all their change on the tombola. Everyone wanted to know who would win the town's Biggest Marrow competition, bag the prize for Floweriest Flower, but most importantly, who would win Best Dog in the annual pet show.

1

And no one was more excited, or impatient, for the pet show to start than Ursula the cat: the newest and  smartest member of the gang known as the Scruffs. Ursula lived in Mr Straw's Perfect Pet shop (he thought he owned them, but he was definitely wrong about that), and right now she was waiting by some hay bales for the rest of her friends, and getting pretty fed up with how late they were.

You see, Ursula had a plan – a plan hatched many weeks ago...

It had been the usual sort of lazy afternoon in the Perfect Pet Shop. Ursula was snoozing on Mr Straw's lap when the telephone rang (Mr Straw had also been snoozing, which was his favourite pastime).

Ring-ring!

The telephone *never* rang, so Mr Straw

jolted awake and leapt out of his chair as if he'd been stung by a wasp, causing Ursula to jump off at the same time.

"Ahem... Hello? The Perfect Pet Shop, Mr Straw speaking, how can I help?" The voice on the other end sounded very official and Ursula sidled up close to listen in.

"Good afternoon, Mr Straw – this is your bank manager speaking. It has come to my attention that you have not paid off your loan this month. You do realize your business and your property are at risk if you don't make the payment?"

"Er . . . yes! Of course! I'll have the money to you directly," blustered Mr Straw.

But when he put the phone down he looked extremely worried.

"How on earth am I going to come up with that sort of money!" he muttered, and sank down into his chair.

Ursula had immediately rushed to tell the other Scruffs what she had discovered.

"I don't think poor Mr Straw has any idea how he is going to pay!" she finished.

"But . . . but this means we could lose our home!" gasped Elvis the chameleon.

"Maybe business will pick up soon?" said Lost the budgie hopefully.

The animals had gazed around their beloved but dilapidated pet shop, with its flea-ridden carpets and dusty merchandise. Mr Straw wasn't going to raise funds by selling a tube of Meaty-Dog toothpaste and some shredded hamster bedding once a week.

"We need to help him get the money," cried Itch.

"My thoughts exactly," Ursula agreed. "And look at this – do you remember we were going to hatch a plan to enter...?"

The animals gathered round and looked at a poster, which had been posted through the letterbox.

"That's the one advertised a few weeks back in the newspaper. There are cash prizes..." murmured Gerb the Gerbil.

"We should definitely enter!" cried Itch the dog. "I know we're not the poshest pets – but with our skills there's no way we won't win SOMETHING."

"Let's do it!" They had cheered.

And that was how Ursula found herself ready to compete in the Much Muddling Town Fete Pet Show with her friends – if the rest of the gang ever showed up. She knew in her heart the chances of the Scruffs winning anything were slim, but Ursula had been practising her cat-ninja display skills for weeks. Maybe, just maybe, the judges would be impressed...

But *where* were the Scruffs? Just then...

"Oi! come back here, you...!"

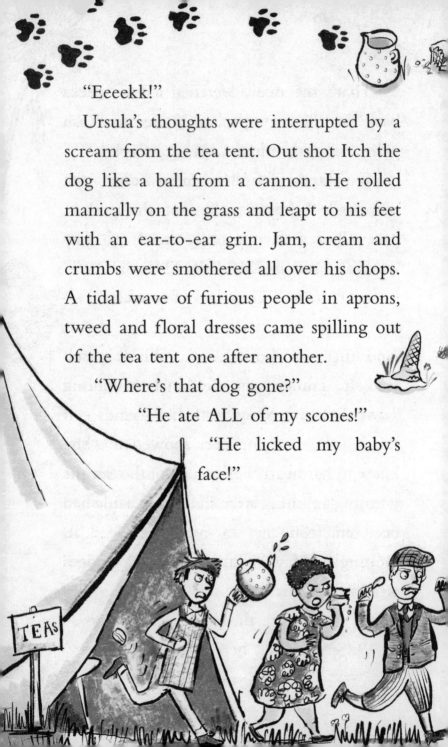

"Eeeekk!"

Ursula's thoughts were interrupted by a scream from the tea tent. Out shot Itch the dog like a ball from a cannon. He rolled manically on the grass and leapt to his feet with an ear-to-ear grin. Jam, cream and crumbs were smothered all over his chops. A tidal wave of furious people in aprons, tweed and floral dresses came spilling out of the tea tent one after another.

"Where's that dog gone?"

"He ate ALL of my scones!"

"He licked my baby's face!"

TEAS

Itch sloped away, towards where Ursula was waiting. Out of sight, behind the bales, he slumped down happily. "I couldn't resist those delicious bakes," he admitted sheepishly. "So ... much ... cream."

"WE ARE LATE FOR THE SHOW!" hissed Ursula. "Where are the others?"

And just then:

"Mummy! I saw a rat – a big rat with ears. It was sucking all the seeds out of Auntie Mavis's tomatoes."

And suddenly there they all were, emerging from the produce tent: Gerb the gerbil ("I'm not a rat!"), Elvis the chameleon and Slug the ... yes, yes, the slug, all looking a bit shell-shocked. Ursula glared at them as Lost the budgie, a confusion of

yellow feathers
wearing a large
pair of glasses, dropped
from the sky and landed in
the hay. *Flump!*

"I got lost," she said.

Ursula took a deep breath. "RIGHT!
Well, now you are all *finally* here, I guess we
can enter the pet show. I'd like to remind

you that the fate of the shop rests on us doing well here today. Itch, I'm assuming Mr Straw is where you left him?"

"Yep!" Itch said. "He's asleep in a deckchair right next to the show ring."

It hadn't been easy for the Scruffs to "persuade" Mr Straw to attend the fete, but Ursula had been determined her plan was going to work. They made sure his alarm was set early, his outfit for the day was ready, his shoes were in a pair and his keys were in the right place.

That morning, under strict instructions from Ursula, Itch had waited by the door, whining and wagging his tail. He had done his best "I'm desperate for a wee" expression whilst holding a lead in his mouth.

11

As soon as Mr Straw had attached the lead
to Itch's collar, he found himself being
dragged all the way to the Much Muddling
Fete.

The other Scruffs had followed at a
distance so as not to be spotted, and once
they'd got Mr Straw to the playing
field they instantly abandoned him in a
convenient spot and went off to explore.
Mr Straw was slightly surprised to be

there, but managed to find himself a cup of tea and a slice of fruit cake, so he settled himself down for the afternoon.

Chapter Two
THE PET SHOW

"Well? What are we waiting for?"

As Ursula had feared, by the time they pushed their way though the queues, the Cleverest Cat contest had already ended. It had been won by a cat who could add up sums by ringing a little bell. "I just cheated!

I always cheat!" the cat was boasting to whoever would listen. But as people are stupid and can't understand cats, she was awarded first prize. Ursula was bitterly disappointed; her cat-ninja routine was far superior. Unfortunately she would now have to rely on the others...

The show began.

First up was the exotic pet bit of the show ... but Elvis had been practising and was a bit TOO good, so the judge didn't notice him.

Then it was the bird show, but Lost didn't stand a chance against the exotic parrots –

although she did get a chance to practise her Filipino with a charming cockatoo named Angelo.

Slug was disappointed to hear that the "small but beautiful" animal contest had been cancelled.

I could have been a contender!

But Gerb, who had been so keen on the pet show idea originally, seemed relieved. "I forgot that I get stage fright, and when I get nervous – I bite."

Then it was time for the most popular contest – the dog show! The tent was buzzing with people. There were no more contests after this. That meant that the Scruffs entire hopes of winning the show – and some prize money to help out Mr Straw – were resting on . . .

Itch.

Ursula gave him a little pat on the back, and said (with as much encouragement as she could muster), "Good luck, Itch! I know you'll do your very BEST."

"OK, OK!" Itch yawned. "Whatever you say!"

A tannoy burst into life:

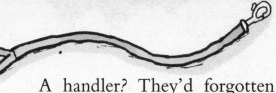

A handler? They'd forgotten all about Mr Straw, who was still dozing in his deckchair. Thanks to an enthusiastic tongue bath from Itch, they managed to get him up and ready, even if he didn't *quite* know what was happening.

There were ten dogs in the ring. People clapped politely as the handlers sprinted around in a circle, their trusty canines padding along beside them, although in Itch's case he was the one leading Mr Straw.

"Hurrah for our canine stars!" cried the announcer. *"And now we have a very special introduction to make — we are honoured to have not one but TWO elite dog-show winners here to guest judge our little show. Their dogs have won TOP DOG at the nation's prestigious TOP PET show three times in a row. Today they are very excited to give one lucky dog and owner here*

a golden token to enter that very competition!
Welcome, Lynn and Lonny!"

Lynn and Lonny stepped in to the ring.
They were dressed smartly in identical black-
and-white suits, Lynn's hair was coiffed to
perfection and Lonny had a little waxed
moustache.

"They don't look thrilled to be here, do they?" whispered Elvis to Ursula, who had to admit that they looked pretty awkward in the scruffy little ring.

Then they got down to business of looking at dogs. Lynn made notes on her clipboard and Lonny stood next to her whispering; they occasionally raised an eyebrow when some dogs barked or jumped up. Then some dogs would get sent out of the ring and the others would stay in for more judging. The Scruffs held their breath as Lonny and Lynn briefly looked Itch over. Ursula snuck up as close as she could to overhear their conversation.

"What a joke! This is what happens when you agree to judge these local shows," Lonny said confidently.

"Hang on a second, Lonny," Lynn said slowly. "That one might just have something." And she signalled to Mr Straw to stay put.

Yesss! Itch had made it into the second round!

Still remaining was a cross-looking pug, a nervous Dalmatian, two yappy Pomeranians, a huge dribbly St Bernard ... and Itch.

"I'm crossing all my fingers," Slug said, sliding up behind Ursula.

"You don't have fingers!" laughed Lost.

"Shh!" Ursula frowned. "This is getting tense!"

Lynn and Lonny started examining each dog more closely in turn. The judges walked around each dog, asking it to sit and then looking at its eyes, mouth and ears. Then, they watched the handler run the dog around the ring. When they came over to Mr Straw and Itch, Lonny just stared incredulously. Then he let out a little snigger, which Itch didn't seem to notice, but Ursula did. The audience seemed to be tittering too. Lynn elbowed Lonny hard in the ribs.

"Do you ... regularly compete in dog shows, Mr, er, Straw?" she asked, examining Itch.

Mr Straw started chuckling. "Ha – not at all! I'm not sure how I got myself into this one, to be honest... But you can see this chap here can't disguise his true colours today! He's a champ."

"Hide . . . his true colours. . ." murmured Lynn. "Yes. . ." She had a funny look on her face. Ursula wondered what she was thinking, but then she seemed to snap out of it and get on with the judging.

Lynn looked in Itch's eyes, his mouth (while holding her breath) and his ears. Then she sent them off for a lap of the ring and discreetly took a wet wipe out of her pocket to clean her hands. Itch marched proudly with head in the air all the way round.

Lynn and Lonny were whispering to each other. "Gerb, can you hear what they are saying?" Ursula asked curiously.

Gerb pricked up his enormous gerbil ears and relayed the conversation:

Lonny: "What's going on, Lynn? Is there a consolation prize for mankiest pet?"

Lynn: "He's the one, Lonny."

Lonny: "Say what!?"

Lynn: *(Harshly)* "Just look at him and his owner. They are just ... perfect."

Lonny: "But..."

Lynn: "Shut up, Lonny. I know best here. We have a winner."

"Are you sure you heard that last bit correctly, Gerb?" Ursula asked, stunned. "Did she say ... a winner?"

Lynn had been handed a microphone.

"The winner is ... Mr Straw with his dog, er ... Itch! This dog demonstrates the ideal characteristics of his, er, breed, and has behaved impeccably."

She strode over to Mr Straw and vigorously shook his hand. "Itch here will get the first prize of fifty pounds and a golden token to enter the Top Dog competition at Top Pet next week – the most elite and prestigious dog show in the world!"

Mr Straw looked baffled, but also quite chuffed. The audience also seemed surprised that an eyepatch-wearing "pirate dog" with matted fur had bagged top prize; but the ins and outs of the dog-show world were a mystery to most people, so they just clapped politely.

"He's a good dog, but I'm still not sure why he won," Mr Straw mumbled. "The other dogs look so much ... cleaner?"

"You're being modest, Mr Straw – cleanliness isn't everything. Itch here is a very *unique* and *special* dog. He has a huge amount of ... potential," Lynn was explaining. "It takes a real expert, like myself or Lonny here, to spot that, but he has raw talent. He could go far, in the right hands."

Itch turned to wink at the Scruffs. "You can rely on me!" he barked proudly, wagging his tail. He jumped up on to an upturned crate to receive his huge red first-place rosette, and Mr Straw was

27

handed the golden
token and the prize
money.

Ursula cheered
the loudest; her plan
had come together
perfectly. She wasn't
quite sure what
had just
happened
or why, but
the important thing was that they had
won fifty pounds for Mr Straw. (Ursula
didn't really know an awful lot about how
much things cost in the human world,
but she hoped that once Mr Straw had
paid his debts, he might have enough left
over for a few tins of her favourite cat
food: Superb Kitty Extra-Chunky Lobster
Delight with Caviar and Brie.) Plus, it

looked like they were all going to the TOP PET show!

Mr Straw headed home happily to celebrate with a cup of tea, and the Scruffs trotted after him. Everyone was cheerful after their unexpected win.

What they didn't notice was that they were being followed...

Chapter Three

LYNN AND LONNY MAKE A VISIT

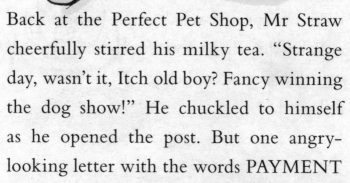

Back at the Perfect Pet Shop, Mr Straw cheerfully stirred his milky tea. "Strange day, wasn't it, Itch old boy? Fancy winning the dog show!" He chuckled to himself as he opened the post. But one angry-looking letter with the words PAYMENT DUE URGENTLY stamped on the front soon wiped the smile off his face. He stared at it for a very long

time, and his shoulders slumped once more.

Ursula sighed. Maybe the fifty pounds prize money wasn't going to be enough after all? She waved frantically at the others.

"Scruffs! We need to have a serious meeting – to the Den!"

The Den was an old rabbit hutch in the back yard of the Perfect Pet Shop. Everyone

SHOW
Cash Prizes
First Prize winners go to
TOP PET the most prestigious
Pet show globally! ☆

New
sunny
seeds
TASTY RODENT
TREATS

Much Maddling
1st
FETE

could just about
squeeze in. Slug took out the
notebook they used to write Very Important
Things in. Being the only member of the
Scruffs who could write, he took it upon
himself to take the minutes.

"First, I'd like to congratulate Itch on
his epic achievement in winning the dog
show today," Ursula started.

They all cheered as Itch pinned his rosette
to the wall.

33

Ursula cleared her throat. "The problem is, we need more money, and soon."

"But what will we *doooo*?" Slug wailed. "I'm just an indoor slug – my earning powers are nil... I haven't even finished writing my romance novel yet."

"All is not lost," said Ursula. "The prize money for the Top Pet Show is a LOT more than fifty pounds. Itch will pull it off!" Although something told her that winning a silly pet show at a town fete was a breeze compared to entering a national competition.

Slug scribbled it all down as quickly as he could.

V. IMPORTANT:
itch must
win Top-Dog
at TOP-PET

"That's it!"

"No pressure then!" Itch said sarcastically. "I mean, I know I was good, but. . ."

Suddenly, Gerb pricked up his ears. "Customers?" he said, "I can hear the doorbell!"

The Scruffs abandoned their meeting and rushed back inside the shop.

Two shadows loitered in the shop doorway. A big black motorhome was parked on the pavement.

"Come in!" Mr Straw called out. "Door's open."

Ting-a-ling.

A couple stepped inside. It was Lynn and Lonny from the dog show.

"We hope you don't mind us popping by," said Lynn, smiling. "Only we thought we should perhaps have a little ... follow-up chat about the Top Pet Show coming up. You will enter, I assume?"

"Oh, er, that..." Mr Straw looked around. "Not sure what I did with the token, now you mention it. Here it is!" He held up the token, which was now covered in dog hair and tea.

Lynn looked worried. "You need to keep that token safe, Mr Straw. It could be your ticket to fame and fortune – with our help of course."

"Your help?" asked Mr Straw.

"Mr Straw, was today your first time at a dog show?" Lonny asked

"It was, yes."

"I see. You weren't prepared, were you?"

"Not at all." Mr Straw was never prepared for anything really.

"As I suspected." Lynn smiled thinly. "Well, we just LOVE judging at these little dog shows," she said. "The big shows with the star dogs can get a little tiring after a while. It's so refreshing to see local talent. Isn't it, Lonny?"

"Sure," Lonny nodded.

"And we saw your very special dog, er, 'Itch', there, and we just said to ourselves . . . he's our winner and we just have to have him, didn't we, Lonny?"

"What?" said Lonny, who had been distracted by a rack of discounted squeaky toys that were shaped like false teeth (and only slightly pre-chewed). "Oh, sure. I mean, yes, dear!"

The animals all gasped.

Mr Straw backed away. "*Have him*? He is most definitely not for sale!"

The animals let out a collective sigh of relief.

"Oh no! Ha-ha-ha!" Lynn laughed. "Did I say 'have' him? I meant *help* him, of course. How silly of me.

We just want to help you win the show!"

"You ... help me?"

"Yes!" Lynn went on, taking Mr Straw by the arm and guiding him to his chair. "You see, we know talent when we see it, and Itch has got it. But he needs guidance. Mentoring. Hair and make-up. A bath or four. But with our years at the top of the dog show game, we could help him realize that potential – and help you win the prize money."

"Oh," said Mr Straw. "I mean, I've been meaning to give him a bath myself..."

Lynn laughed. "Oh, we're not just talking about a bit of a scrub. Though we certainly can't enter him in Top Pet if he's covered in filthy creepy-crawlies..." she said, catching sight of Slug.

"Flippin' cheek!" protested Slug. "I don't creep or crawl... I *slide gracefully.*"

"You need *experience*, Mr Straw," continued Lynn. "Because if you don't have it..."

"You'll lose," Lonny said bluntly. "Whereas we have won the Top Dog competition three times in a row. You do realize that the prize money is quite considerable?"

Mr Straw nodded vaguely. "More than fifty pounds?" he asked.

Lonny chuckled. "Why, yes, you could say that. Top prize is £100,000."

Mr Straw gasped. His eyes glazed over, and the Scruffs knew he was imagining all his financial difficulties disappearing. Ursula couldn't help picturing herself diving into a mountain of Superb Kitty Venison Surprise with Saffron and Truffle Oil.

"Let's say," Lynn went on smoothly, "we

take him to Top Pet for you. Training and
grooming will be included, of course. After
we've worked our magic Itch will be a ...
very different pooch. Then, of course, we'd
be honoured to handle him in the Top Dog
competition for you. We just love the glory
of winning, don't we, Lonny?"

"Yes, Lynn. The glory of winning and,
perhaps, a small share of the winnings? That
seems only fair."

"Of course, of course,"
murmured Mr Straw,
looking dazed.

"I am not
HAVING A BATH!"
whined Itch, who
hated being
brushed or
washed.

"See? He can't

43

wait to get started!" said Lynn, failing to understand Itch's protest.

"Oh come on, Itch!" Ursula frowned. "Our future is at stake here"

"Well," smiled Lynn, taking Lonny's arm. "We'll get out of your way and let you have a little think about it." She handed Mr Straw a business card. "Just give us a call when you've made up your mind."

"Just don't think too long," grinned Lonny on his way out of the door.

After they'd gone, Mr Straw looked over to the counter where the bank statements lay, red, angry and OVERDRAWN. Of course he'd have to call them first thing tomorrow and accept their offer.

Poor Mr Straw. Everything always seemed so overwhelming. He ought to ... zzzzz...

"I'll do it," Itch said dramatically "I'll put myself through the humiliation and

discomfort of being groomed for the sake of our pet shop and our gang. But, on one condition..."

"Yes?" the others asked.

"You *all* have to come to the show as well – and make sure you bring Mr Straw. I don't want them to get too fond of me and not give me back. I am pretty loveable, you know."

"We wouldn't miss it for anything," Ursula purred.

Things were looking exceedingly hopeful, although something was niggling her. Could things be a bit too good to be true? And if they really were top dog-show handlers who could have chosen any dog to take to the show – why choose Itch?!

Chapter Four

THE POOCH-MOBILE

It was the day before the Top Dog competition and the animals were all waiting for Lonny and Lynn to arrive to collect Itch.

Itch was pacing around nervously. "I need to focus," he said gruffly whenever anyone said anything to him.

Mr Straw seemed nervous too. He had washed and even brushed his hair, and was wearing a clean jumper (even if he'd failed to notice it was inside out).

Soon the shiny black motorhome pulled up in front of the shop.

"They're here!" Gerb yelled.

The Scruffs rushed to the window and squashed their noses up against the glass. On the side of the vehicle, Lynn and Lonny had stuck enlarged photos of their faces, and underneath in hot pink script were the words: LYNN & LONNY: 3X WINNERS OF TOP DOG. Their number plate read: D0GZ 4 W1N.

Lynn burst into the shop in a cloud of perfume. "Coo-eee, we're here!! And there's my little superstar!" she cried, walking over to Itch and patting him affectionately.

"I've packed him a bag," Mr Straw said, handing over a battered old carrier.

"Oh, you needn't have bothered, Mr Straw! Lonny and I have everything ready for our special guest!"

Lonny was waiting in the driver's seat of the motorhome with his designer sunglasses on. He jumped out and opened up the side door. "Let me show you around our Pooch-Mobile!" Lynn was saying to Mr Straw. The Scruffs, being nosy, slipped out of the shop and followed quietly behind Itch to get a closer look too.

The inside of the Pooch-Mobile was amazing. There was leopard-print seating, fluffy cushions, sparkling black granite

worktops and pictures of dogs in lighted frames all over the walls. There was an over-stuffed dog-sized couch and a touchscreen TV low to the ground. Copies of *That Hound* magazine and *Doggy Vogue (Dogue)* were piled neatly next to the couch.

"Is all this just for Itch?" gasped Mr Straw.

"Of course!" cried Lynn. "And this is his show wardrobe..." She opened a door and revealed a selection of black and white leads and collars in expensive designer leather. What a contrast to the tangle of leads that Mr Straw had for sale in the shop!

"It's flashy in here, don't ya think?!" Elvis said.

"Personally I think it's a bit tacky," Ursula replied, although it wasn't much different to the way she used to live. She touched her jewel-encrusted collar and remembered with mixed feelings how she had once been

someone's treasured-but-bored house cat.
She was *so over* all of that now; she'd much
rather have friends than her own TV.

"This is where we'll prepare
his special diet," Lynn went on, pulling
out a minibar full of specially
sourced, freshly cooked meats
and doggy treats. Ursula

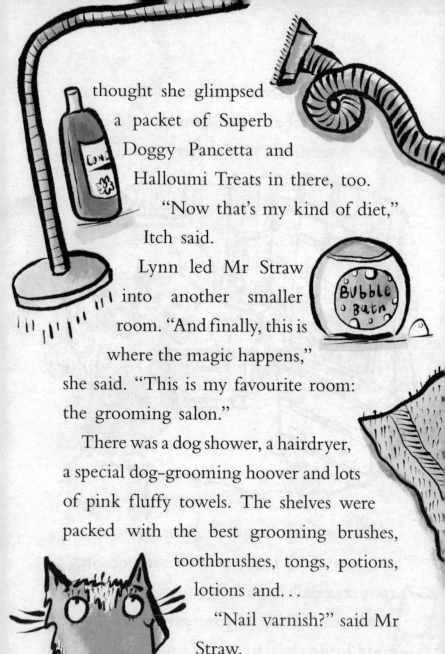

thought she glimpsed a packet of Superb Doggy Pancetta and Halloumi Treats in there, too.

"Now that's my kind of diet," Itch said.

Lynn led Mr Straw into another smaller room. "And finally, this is where the magic happens," she said. "This is my favourite room: the grooming salon."

There was a dog shower, a hairdryer, a special dog-grooming hoover and lots of pink fluffy towels. The shelves were packed with the best grooming brushes, toothbrushes, tongs, potions, lotions and...

"Nail varnish?" said Mr Straw.

"I always think of the little details, that's why we're the best!" Lynn said.

The Scruffs looked horrified. The "salon" seemed more like a pet torture chamber. They all turned to see if Itch felt the same, but Lonny had handed him a bowl of liver parfait with fruity couscous and he'd made himself comfortable on the couch.

"Well, goodbye, Itch," Mr Straw said, patting him on the head. "And don't worry, boy — I'll be coming to the Top Pet Show to watch you perform."

"Ah, yes..." said Lynn, giving Lonny a funny look.

Lonny put his hand on Mr Straw's shoulder "Are you sure you want to bother with that, Mr Straw? You can watch the whole thing on TV. It may make things easier ... for everyone."

"Oh no: Itch is my dog, and I'll be there for him," Mr Straw said firmly. He fished around in his pocket and pulled out the golden token. "But I guess you'll be needing this. . ."

Lynn almost snatched it from him.

The Scruffs watched as the big Pooch-Mobile sped off in the direction of the motorway with Itch staring out the back.

"He'll be just fine," Ursula reassured the others. "Anyway, we'll see him at Top Pet tomorrow."

She just hoped Mr Straw had remembered to put some diesel in his old van.

Chapter Five

TOP-PET CHAOS

TOP✸PET

WHERE TIP-TOP PETS
COME TO SEE WHO'S TOP!

TOP DOG · TOP BIRD · TOP REPTILE · TOP RODENT · TOP CAT

The Scruffs tumbled out of Mr Straw's van after an exhausting journey, looking even more scruffy than usual. "Thank goodness!" cried Lost. "I thought that journey would never-ever end."

"I'm a-feeling carsick," said Elvis.

"Driving isn't Mr Straw's strong point..." agreed Gerb. "Those roads were total mayhem."

"I'm not sure it's any better out here," Ursula warned.

They gazed around. Ahead of them was the main arena, a huge building shaped like a meringue, and surrounding it were hundreds of stalls selling everything pet-related. Then, as far as the eye could see, there were fields of motorhomes, caravans and tents. The gang had never been anywhere so large and chaotic. Mr Straw had already vanished into the thronging crowds.

Everywhere at Top Pet, people were busy, busy, busy. Some were wheeling pets in cages, some were walking around with them on leads or picking up their poop. Others were rushing around shopping, eating, taking snapshots on mobile phones or chatting to their pets. No one noticed the small group of strange-looking animals walking around by themselves.

They passed the stalls: psychic cat healing, dog dentistry, guinea-pig clothing, bird yoga.

"Gerbil nappies? Who'd make their pet wear those?" Gerb asked, disgusted.

GERBIL NAPPY

"How on earth are we going to find Itch in all this?" asked Ursula, looking around but only seeing hundreds of legs.

"Let's ask someone where the show dogs are," Lost suggested. "But it's probably best we stick together. I will definitely get lost."

"Oh, Lost! Cooeee! My friend!" trilled a familiar voice. It was Angelo the cockatoo from the Much Muddling Town Fete. He was perched high on a stand selling parrot toys.

"Are you competing?" asked Lost politely.

"Oh no, we're just here to sell, sell, sell."
Angelo waved at a colourful range of beads and bells.

"We are looking for the show dogs," Ursula explained. "Our friend is competing today."

"Over there." Angelo pointed a wing to the far corner of the car park, where the motorhomes and caravans were lined-up in long neat rows. "Can I interest you in one of these – on the house? This one is yellow – it will match your feathers!"

"Thanks! Erm … I mean, *Salamat!*" chirped Lost, and they trotted off.

"So, this is the *Dog Village,*" Ursula muttered, feeling slightly nervous at being the only cat in the vicinity.

Most dogs were sitting outside their mobile homes or in their pup-tents waiting for their owners to groom them for the main event. All of them already seemed to be perfect examples of what a dog should be: their coats shone brightly and some were wearing dog shoes and hairnets so their feet and fur didn't get muddy.

"Excuse me, do you know where Lynn and Lonny

are parked?" Ursula asked a friendly looking golden retriever. "They're famous dog handlers and they're showing our friend today."

"Lynn and Lonny..." the retriever pondered.

I've heard of them. They haven't been to a dog show in a while though. Old news.

"Really?!" asked Ursula. "But, I thought they were famous!"

Just then Gerb pricked his huge ears and squeaked. "I think I can hear something – it might be Itch! Follow me!"

They wove their way through the parked vehicles to the far end of the car park where they found the Pooch-Mobile parked next to the stinky portaloos. The doors were all shut and the curtains were drawn, but from inside the Scruffs could hear bleeping noises and electronic music followed by the sound of Itch yawning loudly.

"I knew it was him," Gerb said.

Ursula did a ninja leap up to open the door handle "It's locked," she said. "I'll climb up on the roof while the rest of you keep a lookout."

Ursula peered down through the sunroof.

She could see Itch sprawled out on his couch, surrounded by empty plates of food and playing a dog video game.

"Pssst! Itch!!"

"Oh, hi, Ursula!" Itch said, looking up lazily. "Whatcha up to?"

"More like, what are you up to?" Ursula asked. "You're the big star! How are you? Is everything OK?"

"Oh, it's fine. Only, Lynn and Lonny have gone off somewhere," Itch said, yawning again, "and I am all out of Iberico sausage.

Do you think you could get me some more from somewhere?"

"Um, maybe later," Ursula said. "But listen – the rest of the gang are all here and they'd love to say hi."

Itch shrugged. "Not right now. I've got a lot of preparation to do for the show. I mean, Lynn said I have to go for a shower when she returns. A SHOWER. That's what I'm putting myself through to win..."

"Itchy-poo!" Lynn's voice called. "I'm back! I hope you weren't bored!"

"Oh, there she is now," Itch said. "My agent."

Ursula stayed quiet and watched through the sunroof as Lynn unlocked the door and came in.

There you are, my precious little gold mine! Time for your fantastic grooming session. We're going to transform you into a winner today!

she cooed, dangling some chicken liver above Itch's nose...

"In fact, TRANSFORM is definitely the word...

Ha! Follow me…" And with the help of the chicken liver, Lynn ushered Itch into the grooming salon and slammed the door.

"Well!" Ursula scoffed. Itch certainly was developing a diva-like attitude. She dropped off the roof to report back to the others.

"Itch is getting ready," she told them. "He's a bit too busy to come out and say hi right now, but we'll definitely cheer him on in the ring." Her stomach grumbled – it was all that talk of Iberico sausage. "But let's find some lunch first."

Chapter Six

A WORRYING DISCOVERY

The Scruffs raided a rubbish bin for lunch and came up trumps. Ursula had found a half-empty can of tuna, Lost and Gerb shared a packet of nuts and Elvis swiped the grass with his tongue for tasty flies. Slug munched his way through a dandelion leaf.

The others chattered but Ursula was quiet. She couldn't stop worrying that there was something fishy

going on — besides the
tuna. Something that
had been bothering
her all along.

"Just what has Itch
got that the others
haven't, and why do
Lynn and Lonny think he'll
win?" she asked aloud through mouthfuls
of tuna.

Elvis shrugged. "He does have quite a
magnetic personality. . ."

"Charisma," agreed Lost.

"Yes, but. . ." Ursula sighed. "Does no
one think it's weird that they chose him? I
mean — look around. Does he fit in here?"

The Scruffs looked around at the perfect
dogs, including two poodles tied to a trailer,
lapping bowls of cream.

The younger poodle noticed the Scruffs —

she giggled and wagged her fluffy tail in delight. "Dad! Dad! Look!" she yelped "Ugly animals!!"

"EXCUSE ME!" Ursula hissed. "How rude!"

"Oh sorry," said the poodle, turning a little pink. "I didn't think you had feelings."

"What's going on, Chantilly?" asked the older poodle. Then he caught sight of the Scruffs and wrinkled his nose. "What are *you* doing here?" he said suspiciously.

The Top Pet show is for top pets and their friends only.

"We are friends with a top pet," explained Lost. "We're just waiting for our friend Itch to finish his grooming session. He's going to win Top Dog because he's been groomed by professional, Top Dog competion-winning handlers Lynn and Lonny."

"Who are *they*?" asked Chantilly "And anyway, it doesn't matter – your friend can't win because I always win."

The older poodle frowned. "Lynn and Lonny..." he murmured. "Why, they're a blast from the past. I don't think they've won a show for at least six years. Been down on their luck."

"Really?" Ursula asked "But they said..."

"I heard they cheated too, once, and that's why they haven't been on the scene for a while, but that could just be rumours. Someone told me they were having to lower their game these days, doing things like judging small-town shows. Guess they have to make money somehow..."

The Scruffs enchanged worried glances.

"So they're back, are they?" The older poodle went on. "Well, best of luck to them. They'd better have a pretty good entry this year – my petit Chantilly will be hard to beat... What breed is this Itch?"

"Breed!!?" Ursula gasped, laughing.

She saw the poodle was completely serious.

"Yes, you know – what pedigree? Top Dog competitors have to be pedigree." He gave them a curious look. "You can't even enter if you're not."

"Ah, of course, he's a … well, you'll just have to see. Now, if you'll excuse us…"

Ursula said, "we have some urgent business to attend to. I hope you have a fun show," she said to Chantilly.

The Scruffs slipped

behind a tent and
formed a huddle.

"Listen up, Scruffs.
This is not good news.
We all know Itch isn't
a pedigree breed – he's
a mongrel through and
through."

"Why, he's a mixture of who-knows-
what and mayhem thrown in!" Elvis said.
"That Lynn and Lonny must know that
Itch isn't a pedigree breed – so how are
they a-gonna win?"

"By cheating, of course," Slug said. "I
knew there was something a bit slippery
about them."

"I think you're right," Ursula said
thoughtfully. "I've had my suspicions
all along too. The question is – if Itch
isn't a pedigree, then why on earth have

they brought him here to compete?"

No one had any answers, but the Scruffs agreed it was time to dig deeper. And the clock was ticking – soon it would be showtime...

Chapter Seven

THE SCRUFFS INVESTIGATE

The Scruffs crept past the portaloos and back to the Pooch-Mobile. The curtains were still shut, and the sound of rock music echoed through the outside door, which was now ajar.

The Scruffs peered through the gap and saw Lonny was back, lying with his feet up on the couch. He was reading a

magazine and
slurping a pink energy drink.

The door to the grooming salon was still firmly shut, and the Scruffs could hear water running and Lynn talking to Itch soothingly." Not much longer now. You're being a real star..."

Then, harshly: "Lonny! Are you still sitting around doing nothing? In which case, run and fetch me a coffee! Warm milk, *not* hot, and exactly half a sugar."

Lonny leapt guiltily to his feet. "Of course, boss!" he called. Grabbing some change, he dashed out the door towards the coffee stand. He didn't notice the ragtag bunch of small animals hovering in the shadows.

"Here's our chance to look round!" Gerb hopped up the steps on his little legs and ran inside, beckoning the others.

"We need to find some evidence of cheating," Ursula reminded them. "Or of whatever is going on here. Look everywhere, quickly and quietly!"

The Scruffs opened drawers, looked under piles of magazines and riffled through the wardrobe.

"I've found plane tickets and their passports," Lost chirped. Ursula inspected them. "It could just be that they

81

are off on a nice holiday soon..." She looked more closely at the tickets. "Oh. They go tonight, right after the show. That *is* odd..."

"What's this?" Slug said, sliming over to a computer printer. He held up a piece of paper from the print tray.

DOG BREEDS
-R-US

01380

THIS IS TO
Certify
THAT
ITCH
IS A PEDIGREE
'ZERRIER'

"I've never heard of a Zerrier?"

"Quite..." Ursula said sceptically.

Elvis had been busy picking a locked cupboard with his long tongue. "Look in here! I've found a photo album..."

The Scruffs gathered round to take a closer look as Elvis turned the pages.

Lost readusted her glasses. "Is that Lynn?

She looks younger. And there she is with Lonny! That must have been a winning year, look at the trophy and their dog looks super-flash."

"And here's a newspaper article from the time..."

CHEATING SUSPECTED AT TOP-DOG SHOW

Winning couple deny charges, saying there is no evidence that they forged documents. 'All our dogs are 100% pure-bred pedigree and bonafide,' Mrs L. Furrie told our reporter. The documents in question have now gone missing,

Ursula gasped. "I'm not so sure they *were* innocent. Maybe that's why they stopped competing for so long. People must have started to get suspicious. And what are these?" she said, looking through some magazines on the desk.

"Dyeing your dog to look like a panda! Haha! Dyeing your dog to look like a lion, a tiger or a bear!? Oh my!"

There were some very funny photos and some top trend tips.

"But who would want to dye their dog?" Lost asked, astonished.

FANCY PET

IN TREND!
DOG FUR
DYE FUN!

PANDA!

LION

TIGER

"Lynn and Lonny, of course – they want to dye Itch so he looks like a Zerrier, whatever that is…" Ursula gasped.

"Scandalous!" Slug exclaimed.

"Nearly ready, my little superstar!" Lynn's voice came from the other room. "Where is that lout with my coffee?"

"We need to warn Itch," Ursula hissed. "He probably just thinks this is part of his grooming – rather than full-on cheating!"

Just then Lynn emerged from the grooming salon in an apron and gloves and the Scruffs scattered to hide wherever they could. A cloud of steam and a powerful smell like bleach and rose-petals filled the Pooch-Mobile. "I'll just be a few minutes, sweetie pie," she called behind her. "If I want my latte, it looks like I'll have to get it myself."

Lynn carefully locked the door to the salon behind her

and stepped outside to look for Lonny, muttering grumpily.

The sound of a blower and the music playing was all that could be heard from the room. The Scruffs crowded round nervously, listening for signs of distress.

"Itch!" Are you still alive in there?" Ursula mewed through the keyhole.

There was no answer.

"Itch!" The Scruffs shouted together.

"Uh ... hello? I think I dozed off," Itch replied sleepily. "The dryer, it's so ... warm."

"But you hate grooming!" Ursula said.

"I did ... but I'd never experienced this sort of high-quality spa grooming before," said Itch, sounding smug.

"Look, Itch – we think Lynn and Lonny have a plot, to win by cheating," Ursula said.

"Cheating?" Itch was obviously

disinterested. "I don't know what you lot are getting at. I do know that this chicken liver pate is just sublime – smooth, creamy..."

"Listen! You aren't pedigree enough to win the show and they are up to no good!"

Ursula heard Itch growl. "I know what your problem is." "You're jealous because you're pedigree, and you're used to all the attention. Well, now it's my turn!"

I am going to win all the prize money, and the Perfect Pet Shop will be saved. It will all be down to me, and you just can't take it! Let me do my thing!

There was a pause.

"Now, did you bring me that Iberico sausage I asked for?"

"Oh, for goodness' sake!" Ursula mewed. "We're just trying to warn you. If you enter this show it will be under false pretences. I think Lynn and Lonny might be crooks..."

"Uh-huh," nodded Elvis. "And if they get caught, we could all end up rocking the jailhouse..."

At that moment, there was the sound of a key in the lock. The Scruffs made another run for it, this time hurtling out of a window on to the grass below.

"Well, that was a disaster," snapped Ursula as they huddled by the portaloos. "Itch has got too big for his boots – he doesn't want to listen."

"What do we do now?" asked Slug looking up at the sun. "It's late afternoon and nearly Top Dog showtime. And meanwhile Itch has been dyed to look like a Zerrier – whatever that is!"

"We can't let Itch cheat – that would be terrible. And who knows what other sneaky plans Lynn and Lonny have? If they win this show, I don't see them giving Itch back to Mr Straw. I have a very bad feeling about this." Ursula flexed her claws in irritation.

"Ain't nothin' we can do to persuade Itch at the moment," Elvis pointed out. "We need another plan."

"I bet Mr Straw wouldn't be happy about

all this," said Lost thoughtfully. "If only he could see Itch before he enters the arena..."

"Good plan!" cried Gerb. "And if I know Mr Straw he'll be snoozing in a ringside seat... Let's go and find him!"

Chapter Eight

SHOWTIME STRIPES!

The Top Pet main arena was a riot of noise (poor Gerb, with his super-sensitive ears, had to buy some earmuffs to cope). The spectators were itching with excitement for the final and most-important show of the day: the Top Dog competition. There were rows and rows of seats but most of them were already taken; by luck the Scruffs found some empty chairs near the front of the arena and the judges' table.

A big screen was showing past videos of superstar Top Dogs prancing around, and music was blaring from speakers above their heads. A TV crew was there and a presenter was introducing herself.

"Can anyone see Mr Straw?" cried Ursula. But there were so many people it was impossible to find just one.

Three strict-looking judges filed in, the

spotlight following them as they sat down at their table, shuffling their paperwork and opening their clipboards.

"Oh no! It's about to start..." groaned Elvis. "And there's nothin' we can do."

Presenting the competitors!

boomed an announcement. The music changed and lights flared as dogs and their handlers jogged into the arena. Everyone was cheering. There was Chantilly the poodle, swishing her pom-pom tail in excitement, and the kindly golden retriever was there

too, among others. Each dog looked just as preened and glossy as the next.

Just then, Lynn and Lonny entered the spotlight wearing matching pink suits – and so did Itch.

The other dogs in the arena all stared in amazement at their fellow competitor. This was something no one had seen before.

The crowd oohed. The judges gasped and an awed silence fell over the arena.

It was Itch – but not as the Scruffs knew him. For Itch was no longer a dirty brown-grey colour with patches.

Itch was ... STRIPY like a zebra!

His fur had been dyed black and he had white stripes painted all over him.

"Oh my giddy aunt!" Gerb squeaked

"What a shock!" Lost choked

"That isn't ... *Itch*, is it?!" Slug gobbled

"Ain't that unexpected!" Elvis gaped.

Ursula was lost for words.
*Surely no one will fall for this —
will they?*

But Ursula was wrong. She
should have realized: people are stupid.

As each animal lined up, they could hear Lynn explaining.

"Why yes – only one of its kind in the world, although we're looking at breeding. The Zerrier – product of a . . . a rare genetic terrier mutation. Such an honour and a privilege to be presenting him for the first time in such prestigious company. . ."

The judges nodded eagerly, staring excitedly at Itch, who seemed completely unaware of why he was getting so much attention (he obviously hadn't realized the extent of his makeover). He was simply enjoying all the fuss.

"Proof of pedigree?" Lynn was saying. "Why, of course." She handed the judges the fake certificate the Scruffs had seen in the Pooch-Mobile.

The judges barely glanced at it.

"Itch! That certificate is fake!" Ursula

mewed as loudly as she could muster, but her voice was lost in the din of the stadium as hordes of photographers shoved past her to get a snap of the exotic new dog breed.

There was the usual ear and mouth checks, clipboard shuffling and judges conferring. The dogs paraded around the arena to "We are the Champions". Then there was a long and agonizing wait as the judges did one more thorough examination of each dog.

"They are looking but they don't see!" Ursula put her head in her paws.

Ladies and Gentlemen, it is an extraordinary day at Top Pet because this year's tip-top TOP DOG is one-in-a-million, a never-seen-before rare breed. The winner is ITCH the Zerrier – with handlers Lynn and Lonny!

"Whooop!" cheered the crowd.
"Nooooo!" yelled the Scruffs.

Lynn and Lonny high-fived each other and Itch leapt up and down beside them.

"Hey! Where are they going now?" asked Slug.

"They must be going backstage before the prize-giving ceremony," said Gerb. "Come on — all is not lost. Let's follow them."

Slipping through velvet curtains, the Scruffs found themselves in a brightly lit room with more press, photographers and

TV crews swarming around. Itch was in the corner posing for pics and signing autographs.

"That's enough!" said Lonny. "Our superstar is exhausted from performing – no more autographs for now." And he whisked Itch away.

The Scruffs saw Lynn on the other side of the room talking to journalists and live TV crews. "So, Lynn, a surprising win after years away from the Top-Dog podium. Tell us more about your Zerrier. Is it true that he's the first of his kind?"

"Why, yes – an extraordinary feat of breeding and genetics," said Lynn smoothly. "And we quickly realized we were on to something special. We wanted to wait until the world was ready for something so unique. He's spent years training for this day."

"Excuse me!" cried a frantic-looking dog breeder at the front. "Would you ever consider selling your Zerrier? I would pay any price..."

A sinister-looking smile lifted Lynn's lips.

TOP ⭐ PET
BACKSTAGE
PASS

"I could never part with my darling Zerrier – not unless I was sure he was going to a *very* good home. And, of course, if the price was right..."

What? They were going to sell Itch? Unacceptable.

"And what will you do with the Top-Dog prize money?"

"We were thinking a holiday to the Caribbean..." Lynn said dreamily.

Just then, Lonny appeared with Itch, and to the horror of the Scruffs they saw the dog breeder advancing, his hands full of cash, talking rapidly into Lonny's ear.

Gerb took off his earmuffs to listen.

"Oh no," he whispered. "They've accepted the offer. They've sold Itch!"

"I knew it!" groaned Ursula. "They must be planning to sell quickly before the dye wears off – and then do a

runner with all the prize money."

"But Itch isn't theirs to sell!" cried Lost. "Mr Straw would never stand for this!"

"Where *is* Mr Straw?" said Elvis, so anxious that he forgot to drawl. "We need to find him."

"And we don't have much time..." groaned Slug, nodding to the entrance to the arena. Lynn was leading Itch away for his victory lap – and yet again there was no way to warn him of his fate.

Chapter Nine

WET PET HEROES

Ursula rallied all the Scruffs around her. "Come on, gang!" she cried. "We need to think like troopers. Think like the old Itch we used to know – he would never let this happen. We need a new super-dooper Scruffs plan. We've got to reveal the real Itch to everyone – or we'll lose him for ever."

Everyone thought hard.

"If it's just dye," said Ursula thoughtfully, "then it must wash out."

"If only we could give him a bath," muttered Elvis. "In front of everyone."

"Yes! Genius!" Ursula said. "If only we were outdoors and it was raining. But we're indoors and it won't rain ... unless..."

Ursula looked up at the ceiling.

"I've got it!" she said. "Listen up, this is the *Save Itch Plan*! Gerb, run fast to the Pooch-Mobile and collect all the important evidence that points to the cheating. Elvis,

find Mr Straw and bring him here. Check all over for him – he must be holed up somewhere, probably asleep. Slug, stay here with me and keep an eye on Itch and that despicable pair. And, Lost, I have a special job for you... We need to make sure they don't get away with this."

As the Scruffs bounced into action, the announcer started up again.

Ladies and gentlemen, it's the moment we have all been waiting for! This year's unique Top Dog is 'Zerrier' Itch handled by Lynn and Lonny.

Lynn, Lonny and Itch strutted around waving at the cheering crowds.

"And now, for the presentation of the trophy – and let's not forget the prize money!" chortled the judge.

Meanwhile, above everyone's heads, a scruffy budgie flew round and round. Lost was very good at flying in circles but she wasn't very good at finding things. On the third lap of the stadium she finally spotted it: the very important button she had been looking for. But on closer inspection, she saw it was locked firmly behind a glass case.

IN EVENT OF FIRE, BREAK GLASS.

Tap! Tap! Tap! She used all her strength to try and break it.

Tap! Tap! Tap! It was no use. Lost's little budgie beak wasn't strong enough.

Who has the strength to break glass like that? Certainly none of the Scruffs, Lost thought to herself. Maybe someone else could help? Then an unusual thing happened – Lost had a brainwave!

"Angelo the cockatoo!"

Through gasps of breath, in broken Filipino, Lost managed to explain to Angelo what was happening, and miraculously Angelo understood. "You want me to make it rain?! How?!"

"Follow me!" Lost chirped

Angelo was used to cracking nuts, and he broke the glass cover easily with one efficient tap of his steely beak. Lost yanked down the button.

The sprinklers were on! Angelo stretched out his wings happily as the water sprayed down. "It's like the rainforest in here now."

"Thanks, Angelo, you're a star! If you ever need the Scruffs gang to help *you*, we'll be there!"

Water, water everywhere! Lynn and Lonny pulled their jackets over their heads. The judges sheltered under their clipboards. The pampered show cats hissed angrily and fled for cover. The show goldfish ... didn't seem all that bothered, to be honest.

Itch was now standing on the podium and he was getting wettest of all.

TOP-DOG
TOP★PET

Lost flew over to where Ursula and Slug were sitting under a chair and watched the spectacle unfold.

"Not *another* wash!" Itch was complaining. At his feet a puddle of black water had pooled. He shook himself vigorously, sending a spray of hair dye to splatter Lynn and Lonny's pink outfits and the judges' faces.

"Oh my goodness!" shouted a boy in the crowd. "That dog is ... changing!"

Everyone rubbed water from their eyes as they turned and stared. The crowd gasped. Lonny and Lynn cowered. Ursula, Lost and Slug cheered. Itch was back to his true self.

Finally, someone got the sprinklers turned off, but Lynn and Lonny were still standing there frozen to the ground in shock, their clothes dripping.

The judges looked incredibly cross. "This Zerrier is not a Zerrier at all!"

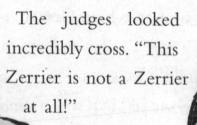

Itch, who had been confused about all the gunk dripping off him, glared at Lynn and Lonny. Why had they covered him in some sort of black gloop? What was wrong with his actual fur?

"Ergh!" said one of the Judges. "What *is* that dog?! That's no Zerrier! It's not even a terrier!"

It was at that moment Gerb and Elvis returned. Gerb was

carrying an empty box of hair dye. "I found this!"

"Good work!" Ursula picked up the box and with a loud *ME-OW*, ninja kicked it through the air and so it landed at the judge's feet.

A judge picked up the box and scrutinized it. "Hair dye?" she hissed. Lynn and Lonnie cringed.

"I should have known," muttered the judge. "You pair were never to be trusted. On seeing this evidence, Lynn and Lonny, you will be banned from competing ever again." She looked over his glasses at them. "You have brought shame on yourselves." Lynn started sobbing but Lonny was backing away, his eye on the trophy...

Itch turned his head and saw Lonny grab the cheque and the trophy off the table. He was going to make a run for it.

"Grrrrr! Woof! Thief!"

Itch leapt off the podium and charged

towards Lonny. He jumped on to his back and knocked him flat, face down in a dirty puddle!

Then he sat on him.

"Get ooooff!" shouted Lonny as the audience booed. The rest of the Scruffs all ran into the arena and piled on too.

"He's not going anywhere!" Ursula mewed. "Not now the Scruffs are all in it together!"

Chapter Ten

THE SCRUFFS GET FAMOUS!

The police came and escorted Lonny and Lynn away.

> Could the owner of the stray animals please come into the arena?

Mr Straw bumbled in. He looked very concerned. "I was tricked by those cheats," he told the judges. "I'm sorry it caused so much trouble. I would have stopped the whole debacle sooner, but Lonny locked me

in a portaloo. He told me it was a waiting room for VIP dog owners."

HELP!

Poor Mr Straw.

"I found him in a toilet right next to the Pooch-Mobile," explained Elvis to the other Scruffs. "I think he must-a been there the whole time."

The judges were sympathetic. "You should be very proud, sir. Your dog Itch here caught the criminal cheats... Is that your cat, gerbil, chameleon and budgie too?"

Hello! And me, SLUG,

Slug said, although they couldn't hear him, of course.

"Er, yes they're mine – although I'm not sure how they got here..." He scratched his head.

The judges formed a huddle and spoke in urgent whispers. Then, the head judge grabbed a microphone. "I have spoken with my colleagues, and we are in agreement. Itch here may not be a Zerrier and he may not be a pedigree. In fact, this is the first time an animal this scruffy has ever entered the Top Pet arena. But, for his bravery and his quick thinking, we would like to recognize that Itch really is a true hero – and a winner."

The crowd went wild.

"Hurrah for Itch!"

The head judge held up a hand for silence. "We would have lost both the historic Top Dog Trophy and the good name of the prize would have been dragged through the mud, were it not for you and your pets, Mr Straw. And so we would like to compensate you."

And that was how Mr Straw got given a cheque, as the crown roared with approval. It wasn't as much as the fabled Top Dog prize money, but it was enough to pay off his debts, and there would be a little left over for treats for all the Scruffs.

The TV presenter couldn't get enough of Itch. "What a great story," she gabbled. "From hero to zero, then zero to hero! Zebra dog saves the day!"

Mr Straw and the Scruffs enjoyed the rest of the afternoon at the Top Pet Show being given the VIP treatment. And Ursula didn't mind one bit about

Itch taking all the glory, because she was just glad to have him back. He didn't demand sausage or boast about how he saved the day (well, not too much). He just wagged his tail and said to all the Scruffs, "I couldn't have done it without you, and especially you, Ursula."

When they finally all got back to Perfect Pet Shop it was very late, but soon they were all cosy and warm and stuffing themselves with treats.

Mr Straw brought down a dusty old television from his flat to the shop. "You're famous, Itch old boy!"

The Scruffs sat together and watched the events at Top Pet unfold once more on the telly. Itch laughed so much at himself with his stripes that he snorted all his dinner out his nose. They all gasped at Lynn and Lonny's interview, and booed at Itch winning then losing. They stared as the news replayed all the action of Itch chasing and catching Lonny in slow-mo! Then there was an interview with a judge saying how nothing like this had ever happened before in the history of Top Pet, how it was even more dramatic than the Great Parakeet Heist of 1983, and how Itch saved the day and really was the Top Dog in many ways.

"Yippie!" cheered the Scruffs.

"And now for something completely different," the presenter was saying.

"We've seen cheating and winning here today at the Top Pet, but have you ever

YIPPIE!

seen a dancing and
singing chameleon?"

All the Scruffs stared at
Elvis in disbelief. He winked
back. Elvis the chameleon was there on TV,
doing his old rock-star impersonation.

"Well, wasn't that something?!" the presenter giggled. "We've just been told that video has gone viral on the internet... Someone else is famous!"

The Scruff all looked over at Mr Straw to see his reaction, but he was snoring away, sound asleep. Well – it had been a very, very, busy day!

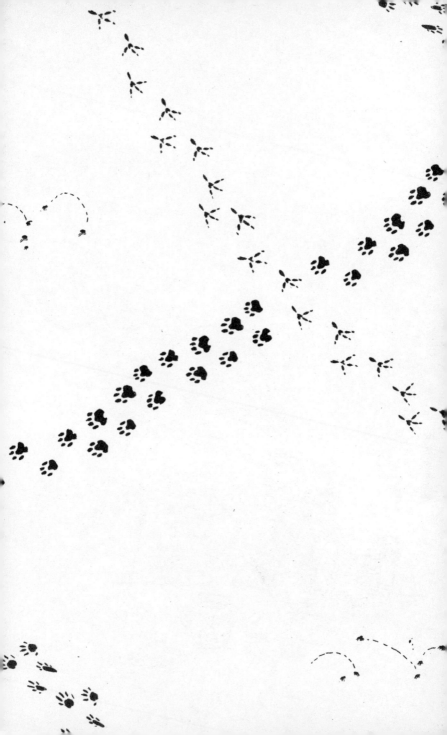

Read
The Scruff's
first hilarious
adventure!

Hannah Shaw is an award-winning author and illustrator of young fiction and picture books. Her books include Stan Stinky, Sewer Hero and Stan Stinky vs the Sewer Pirates as well as Bear on a Bike and School for Bandits. Hannah's illustrations can be seen in books by other authors such as Gareth Edwards' The Disgusting Sandwich and the Sophie stories by Dick King-Smith. She lives on the outskirts of a friendly Cotswold town with her scruffy family and her old smelly dog. She has at least eight unofficial pet slugs who like to glide around her kitchen at night.

Also available by Hannah Shaw...

Meet Stan Stinky – the unluckiest rat in the sewer. But when UNCLE RATTS and his sidekick, ROACHY the cockroach, disappear, Stan must become an ADVENTURER, SURFER and SEWER HERO to save them!

Stan Stinky wants to be a DETECTIVE, but the sewers are crime-free. Until … PIRATES arrive and steal the town's treasures! Can Stan solve the mystery before it's TOO LATE?

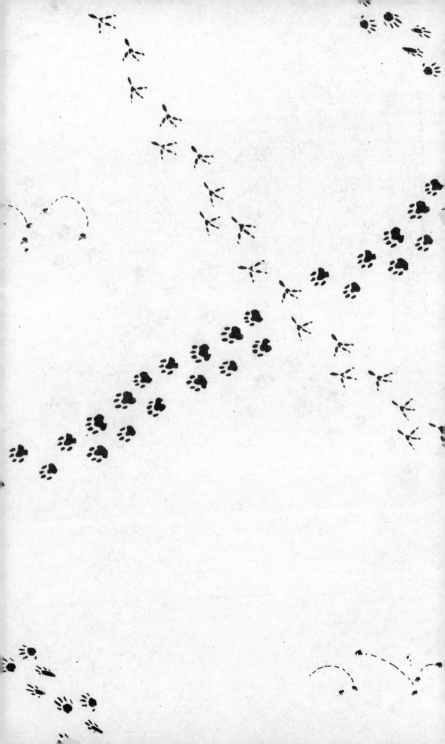